DUDLEY SCHOOLS
LIBRARY SERVICE

KU-394-303

PLANT WORLD

by Paul Collins

pencils by Matt Lin

inks by Aaron Lin

Schools Library and Information Services

S00000734471

All rights reserved.
This 2010 edition published in the United Kingdom by
Scholastic Ltd
Book End
Range Road
Witney
Oxfordshire
OX29 0YD

First published in 2007 by
Macmillan Education Australia Pty Ltd.

Copyright © 2007 Laguna Bay Publishing Pty Ltd.
www.lagunabaypublishing.com

All rights reserved.

Text by Paul Collins
Cover design by Allison Parry
Pencils by Matt Lin
Inks by Aaron Lin
Design by Matt Lin/Goblin Design

No part of this publication may be reproduced, stored in a
retrieval system, or transmitted, in any form or by any means,
electronic, mechanical, photocopying, recording or otherwise,
without the prior permission of the publisher. This book remains
in copyright, although permission is granted to copy pages
where indicated for classroom distribution and use only in the
school which has purchased the book, or by the teacher who has
purchased the book, and in accordance with the CLA licensing
agreement. Photocopying permission is given only for purchasers
and not for borrowers of books from any lending service.

Out of this World: Plant World
ISBN 978-1407-11857-4

Printed by Ashford Colour Press Ltd

1 2 3 4 5 6 7 8 9   0 1 2 3 4 5 6 7 8 9

DUDLEY PUBLIC LIBRARIES

L

734471   Sch

J

S   P   A   R   T   A   N

Contents

Characters

Spartans

Perry

Perry tries to be sensible – he really does.
But he can't say no to an adventure.

Fasool

Fasool is a hot-head. He often leads Perry into trouble –
if Perry doesn't lead him there first.

Sergeant Zach

Perry's Uncle, he is one of the troopers who
patrol *Spartan*. He tries (but fails) to keep
the boys out of strife.

Snookian

Mardi

Mardi is an orphan from planet Snook. She's tough
as old boots – and the most loyal friend ever.

Other Folk

Florians

Native inhabitants of the planet Flora.

Diesel Halftone

A Spartan bully, known more for his
muscles than his brain-power.

Ecori

A humanoid race, who do
the hard work on Flora.

chapter 1

Off the Hook

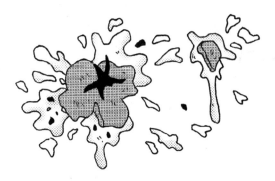

"**Y**ou and your 'let's get something to eat'," Perry complained to his friend. He scrubbed at the sludge mark on the collector tub.

Vac-bots could have been used to clean the tubs, but the job was kept for people who broke the spaceship rules. There was never a shortage of them.

More tubs, having just dumped their vegetable waste, queued to be cleaned.

Fasool pressed a release stud. The tub, now clean, rolled into a chute. Another tub took its place. "How was I to know Sergeant Zach was keeping an eye on us? Sometimes it's a curse that he's your uncle. He doesn't miss a trick."

Perry nodded grudgingly. It was true. Uncle Zach kept a constant eye on him. Which meant if Perry and Fasool put a foot wrong, they were usually caught.

Something went 'splat!' beside their heads. The rotten berrie-berrie pulp spread across the tub's shiny surface like thick green slime.

"Haw haw haw!" laughed Diesel Halftone. Several others sniggered.

Perry silently counted to ten. If you showed a reaction to comet-for-brains like Diesel it only encouraged them.

Fasool obviously disagreed. Already he had his hand filled with decaying vegetable matter. He swung it back and let loose.

"Quick, behind the tub!" Fasool yelled.

Already a barrage of refuse was hurtling across the two lines of collector tubs. It seemed the air was raining overripe fruit and vegetables. Tubs on both sides rocked from the onslaught.

"Why did you have to start this?" Perry seethed. "We were almost finished."

"Me?" Fasool squealed, ducking a squishy banana. "That space-brain Diesel started it."

Fasool stood, lobbed the last of the tub's decent ammunition – a sloppy tomato –

and quickly squatted as five projectiles hurtled overhead. They flattened against the wall and slid like vomit.

"He did it deliberately, knowing we were nearly out of here. It'll take us hours to clean up this mess."

"Maybe he's not as stupid as everyone says he is," Fasool conceded.

Perry glared at him. "I could say something but I won't."

"Look, they've stopped."

Perry poked his head above the tub.

02:15:0021

Diesel and his friends were rushing about like vac-bots, sweeping, rubbing and shovelling up the mess along their line. They would have it spotless within five minutes.

Fasool looked at the wall timer. "Inspection time in 20 minutes," he groaned.

"You were right," Perry said. "They timed it so it'll look like we've been messing about. And if we don't get cleaned up before inspection, we're stuck here until the next shift."

"One of these days I'd like to get the better of that lunkhead Diesel," Fasool said. "Just for once."

"Well you won't if you keep taking his bait," Perry said. "We'll never get this mess cleaned up in time."

Tidying up the fruit and vegetables that plastered every surface of their line took 15 minutes. It put them way behind schedule. Diesel's crew only had two tubs left.

Fasool gritted his teeth. They had five tubs left to clean. The smell was gut-wrenching.

"Just as we entered orbit above Flora, too," Perry said.

"I saw a virtual of it," Fasool said. "It's... well, out of this world."

"Out of this reality," Perry corrected. "I saw it too. Did you see the huge pores on its outer leaves? They looked like craters. They say Flora is a giant cosmic plant that took root on a stray moon and kept growing."

Fasool nodded excitedly. "Flora lives on space matter sucked in by its cosmic ray sponges. And the moon it grows on used to have an ancient civilisation in its catacombs."

Perry shook his head in wonder. "I'd kill to take a look around in all those caves."

"You won't get to visit Flora by chattering like monkeys," bawled a voice Fasool knew well.

"No sir, Sergeant," Fasool said. He scrubbed a little harder.

Diesel made a great show of thumping a stud. He and his crew stood back as their last tub slid smoothly down a chute. Diesel slapped his hands. "All finished, Sergeant Zach," he crowed.

"Stand easy," replied the sergeant.

Perry and Fasool stood. That's when they noticed Mardi behind the trooper. She came from a mining world called Snook. Mining was a dangerous occupation there, because the rocks zipped and zapped across the planet's surface, like billiard balls. Snookians rock-hopped with grappling units.

Mardi winked conspiratorially.

Sergeant Zach looked back at her suspiciously, but Mardi's face was suddenly deadpan.

02:25:002

He lowered his voice so only Perry and Fasool could hear. "It seems your friend here thinks you'd be better punished if you were down on Flora."

Perry nudged Fasool and his huge smile disappeared. "Gosh, Uncle Zach. With friends like Mardi we don't need enemies."

"Keep your voice down," Sergeant Zach said. He looked meaningfully at Diesel and his team. "You're off the hook because Mardi here," he hooked a thumb over his shoulder, "has traded some time on your behalf."

Fasool glared at Mardi. Trading time was a serious business. Sometimes you could trade an hour of scrubbing a floor and wind up owing an hour washing out the sewage ducts.

"Don't look so glum," Sergeant Zach said. "You're heading for Flora, but not solely for entertainment purposes." He looked around to make sure Diesel and his crew were still standing to attention. "The Florians are near-human, but a little... different. They run a pretty tight place down there, so you'll need to watch your ps and qs."

"We'll be good," Fasool gushed.

"I doubt it," Sergeant Zach drawled.

chapter 2

The Plant World

Sergeant Zach talked on, explaining the life forms on Flora. "There's a second non-human but humanoid race called the Ecori. They're sub-intelligent and docile. They do most of the cleaning and basic maintenance on Flora, as well as farming. Droids are Flora's military. We've been asked by the League of Social Conscience to investigate slavery complaints against the Florians."

Fasool began to speak, but Sergeant Zach kept going. "Trouble is, *Spartan* is trying to set up trade negotiations. And if we waltz in there making accusations, we're out on our ears. That plague we had 50 years ago just about wiped out our farming pods. Flora's strain is resistant to any bugs known to us. Our future could well depend on the plant world."

"A tricky situation, Sergeant," Fasool said.

"Be quiet, Fasool," Sergeant Zach growled. He glanced over at Diesel and the others. They were getting impatient but knew better than to show it. He turned his attention back to Perry and Fasool. "I want you two to nose around and pick up any information you can and report directly back to me. We know the Florians are guilty of all sorts of humanitarian failures but we need hard evidence to present to the League." He pursed his lips. "Most societies ignore kids –"

"Don't we know that," Fasool quipped.

"Shut up, Fasool. As I was saying, you'll be better spies than anyone on my team." Sergeant Zach shook his head. "Fasool, Perry, I'm letting you off lightly this time. Keep safe down on Flora. At the first hint of trouble, you get yourselves back on Spartan."

"Yessir," Perry said. "You can count on us."

"Wait," Sergeant Zach added. "If I catch you boys ever going planet-side without permission – even if it is to rescue a friend – you'll be on permanent tub duty."

Before Perry could defend the charge, Fasool saluted. The others followed suit.

Sergeant Zach turned his attention to Diesel and his team. "Right, you two. What are you waiting for? Get over here and clean out these tubs. MOVE IT!"

"But, but..." Diesel stuttered.

"NOW!" bawled Sergeant Zach.

Perry waved to Diesel and grabbed Fasool. They ran helter-skelter down the companionway. Mardi was close behind.

They didn't stop running until they reached a Dial-a-Destination jump gate.

"Why do I always get the shivers around these things?" Mardi wondered aloud.

"They're clear of the latest virus," Fasool said. "I heard it on the comm.stat."

Perry punched a sequence and stepped back. Not that that would save him if the jump gate decided to play up and send him into space.

The DAD whirred and clicked, just as it should.

Fasool beamed. "Today's our lucky day."

They all stepped forward. Perry reached out and hit the 'activate' stud. It pinged. Then they were gone.

The three youngsters brushed aside some purple foliage and stepped out of a Florian jump-gate. Their first thought was that they had materialised inside a giant flower. Flora of every shape and colour imaginable hung from each surface. They looked up and saw a glowing hologram, floating just above their heads.

Perry and Fasool's mouths gaped.

"Wow," said Fasool. "It looks so real you could touch it."

The shimmering hologram was a true-to-life image of *Spartan*. None of them had seen anything like it. The colony craft was a hollowed-out asteroid the size of a small planet.

The sheer enormity of it was overwhelming. Inside that peanut-shaped asteroid was the universe's most diverse cultural mix. Some called *Spartan* a living museum. It contained beings from well over 50 planets, plus flora and fauna from every planet they had visited. Many species were housed cryogenically as well, in case they became extinct and had to be reintroduced to their homeworld.

Mardi stifled a yawn. "I still say it looks like a peanut," she said. "Anyway, let's investigate Flora. Looks like we've landed at a marketplace."

Perry and Fasool lingered a moment longer, then hurried to catch up with Mardi, who was heading towards the market stalls.

"I really hope *Spartan's* cleared a line of credit with Flora," Perry said, checking he had his credit wafer.

Mardi pointed at all the Spartans bartering with the Florian merchants and their staff. "We're in trouble if we haven't," she said.

Everywhere they looked, aliens from every planet they had ever been to were trying out the Florian cuisine. Most had come from *Spartan*, of course.

"It's a bit pongy," Fasool noted.

"Says you," Mardi said, wrinkling her nose. "In case you haven't realised, you guys didn't change before jumping over."

Fasool's face fell. "Oh-my-stars." He took a whiff of his coverall and wheeled about in mock swoon.

"Stop it," Perry hissed. "The locals will think we're rude."

"And they'd be right," Mardi observed.

"Anyway," Perry continued, "we blend in, smelling like this. Hey, the beings behind those stalls must be Ecori. Look at their tufted ears and big sad eyes."

"They look as sad as half-grown pandas out of Old Earth's ancient past," Fasool said.

"Let's get acquainted," Mardi said. "That one over there doesn't look too happy, poor thing. See how his ears are pointed down?"

"I wouldn't be too happy if I looked like an extinct animal," Fasool said.

They made their way toward the sad-looking Ecori's stall. They hadn't quite reached it when a shrill bell rang across the marketplace. Beings everywhere stopped what they were doing.

"Um, was it something I said?" Fasool asked.

chapter 3

Imprisoned

Every Florian in the marketplace suddenly became dormant. They didn't fall. Rather, they wilted. Three uniformed guard droids surrounded each one.

"I thought Uncle Zach said Flora was resistant to our bugs," Perry said.

Aghast, Fasool looked down at himself. "Maybe we should've changed after all."

The sad-faced Ecori offered Fasool a piece of what looked like flower pulp. "Taste like your honey. Only more nutrient," the Ecori said.

"Er, what about all the Florians?" Fasool asked.

"This their siesta time," the Ecori explained in stilted Spartan. "It happen every five hour. Ecori not know why."

"Cool," said Fasool, munching.

"What's so cool about flopping into a trance-like state every five hours?" Mardi asked.

"No, I mean the flower pulp's cool. Falling about the place is a pain."

The three wandered about. It seemed everything went on as usual, although no Ecori or tourists were allowed near the Florians while they were dormant. The guard droids made sure that everyone kept their distance.

Half an hour later a siren blared and the Florians awoke. They looked like flowers reviving after a blistering hot day followed by heavy rainfall.

"Let's see if sad-ears knows anything about this," Perry muttered.

"Maybe a bribe would help,"

suggested Fasool.

"Wait a minute –" Mardi began.

But Fasool wasn't listening. Back at the sad Ecori's stall he offered the stallholder a chunk of Spartan confectionery. Immediately a hand swept the sweet from the Ecori's grip. The Ecori squeaked and cringed back.

Fasool whirled about. A male Florian swung his hand across the stall, scattering its contents. The Ecori shrank in fear.

"Settle down," said Fasool. He blocked the Florian, who was about to up-end the entire stall.

Mardi jumped in between Fasool and the Florian. "Remember what Sergeant Zach said," she warned Fasool.

Fasool looked up at the Florian. It wasn't as though he wanted to take on a creature twice his size, but…

Before he could shove Mardi aside the Florian's droid guards arrived.

"Alien food is poisonous for Ecori," one of them explained. "Your people were informed of this."

Mardi thought back to the information she had memorised. Sure enough, she remembered being told that. But Perry and Fasool had been in detention during the comp-tute.

"We weren't told," Fasool said.

"You are in breach of regulation five-zero-six, subset two," the droid told them. "Ignorance is no defence. Arrest them."

More droid guards fanned out around them. Several Spartan tourists hurried over to help the kids, but an officer ordered them back.

Then the guards simply locked their arms around Perry, Fasool and Mardi and frog-marched them off to jail.

"Call Sergeant Zach!" Perry yelled, as his feet scrabbled in thin air.

They were taken down paths that wound through vast tracts of tilled land. They passed through chambers with luminous fungi growing on the craggy walls, and down wide, furrow-like passages that were lit by overhead solar-powered lights. They marched alongside rows and rows of vegetables – more vegetables than the Spartans knew existed.

Finally they arrived at the dungeons. These were dried-out plant cells. The droids threw the three prisoners into a single cell. A droid pressed a button and thin laser beams zig-zagged across the entrance. There was no mistaking the fact that if Perry, Fasool or Mardi touched those lasers they would be fried.

"Well, that was educational," Fasool said when the guards left.

"Nice one," Mardi said. "We'd been here just over half an hour and you managed to breach one of their strictest regulations."

"How was I supposed to know?" Fasool demanded.

"Well, if you hadn't been such a space-cadet, you wouldn't have been scrubbing out collector tubs when the comp-tute was on."

"All right, you two," Perry said. "Uncle Zach will sort this mess out sooner or later."

"Sooner rather than later," Mardi growled. "I feel as though I've been buried alive in here."

Sergeant Zach arrived within half an hour. He shook his head. "Can't I trust you boys to behave yourselves for five minutes?" He gave Mardi a scathing stare. "I had hoped you would be a calming influence on these two. It appears that I was wrong."

"It wasn't our fault," Fasool said.

"Where have I heard that before?" Sergeant Zach said. He seemed to have aged within the past hour or two. "I'll see what I can do. The Florians have already lodged a complaint with the captain. It's going to hold back our trade negotiations, that's for sure. In the meantime, sit tight."

The kids watched Sergeant Zach leave.

"Sit tight, he says," Fasool mumbled.

"As though we're going to run a marathon," Mardi added.

Perry nudged Mardi. "Someone's coming."

"Your uncle doesn't mess around," said Fasool.

But it wasn't Sergeant Zach. Four droid guards were dragging two hapless victims between them. They tossed the small Ecori into a cell and activated the laser beams.

When the droids had left, Perry called out to the two Ecori prisoners. "Hiya. I'm Perry, this is Fasool, and Wonder-gal here is Mardi."

The Ecori looked bedraggled. Nonetheless, they introduced themselves as Asla and Tuskan.

"What are you here for?" Perry asked.

The Ecori didn't answer at once. Finally, Asla said, "We have been condemned to death for calling for Ecori freedom."

Fasool frowned. "Aren't you free? What's stopping you from moving on?"

Asla and Tuskan looked at one another and their ears dropped. "It is forbidden," Tuskan said. "Many of our siblings would be imprisoned if we fled."

Mardi put her hands on her hips. "That's not right."

Perry wore a worried expression. Mardi was almost as bad as Fasool when it came to getting into trouble. "There's not much we can do about it, Mardi."

"You forget why we're here," Mardi snapped. "These Ecori are all the proof *Spartan* needs of slavery on Flora."

"Er, in case you've forgotten, we're sort of stuck here ourselves," Fasool said.

"Oh?" Mardi asked.

chapter 4

Fugitives

"**T**he grappling unit," Perry said, smacking his forehead with relief.

"Never leave home without it," Mardi said, patting her back.

"I wonder what the punishment is for escaping lawful custody?" Fasool worried.

"Not as bad as what Asla and Tuskan are facing," Mardi said. She turned to the Ecori. "If we can spring you, would you come with us?"

"Spring?" Asla asked.

"Free you," Mardi explained. "If we can get you to Spartan, our captain might be able to stop what's been going on here."

"Mardi!" Fasool hissed. "We're supposed to be undercover."

"Oh, really?" Mardi replied. "So undercover we're down in a dungeon."

The two Ecori whispered together. Tuskan said, "This dungeon in sepal. This is base of main flower and protect the bud. Most secure. The wall are solid hollifer, the smoothest bark in universe. No-one ever escape."

"I'm not talking about climbing anything," Mardi said, aiming her collapsible harpoon. "Are you with us or against us?"

Asla and Tuskan touched their foreheads together. Then Asla said, "We have decided. We shall go with you."

"No time like the present," Mardi said. She stalked about the cell, scrutinising the cathedral-like ceiling. "There's a likely spot. Has a small ledge, and an opening."

"For bee," Asla explained. She didn't look happy.

"Honey pot here we come," Mardi said. She looked elated as she aimed her harpoon. It wasn't often these days that she got a chance to use her grappling unit. She pressed a stud and launched

the harpoon. True to its mark it struck the ceiling above the opening.

Perry and Fasool clutched onto her utility belt and Mardi hoisted the three of them up to the ledge. Moments later she dropped into the Ecoris' cell, and shot back up to the ledge with them dangling from her waist.

Asla and Tuskan chirruped to each other. They had just done something they thought impossible: escaped from a Florian dungeon.

A bee landed on Fasool's shoulder. He brushed it off.

Another one landed on his arm.

"No kill bee," Asla cried.

Too late. Fasool had swiped it off and it fell into the gloom.

The next moment a swarm of bees had descended upon them.

Mardi reeled in her harpoon and broke the Snookian golden rule: never shoot your grappling unit on impulse. The harpoon struck the stem of a towering plant. "Hold tight, everyone!"

Clenching their eyes shut against the buzzing bees, the two Spartans and two Ecori clustered around Mardi.

The grappling unit whirred and buzzed louder than the frenzied bees. The load – five humanoids – was way over its safety levels. They swung across a maize field, sweeping just centimetres across the tallest sheaves.

"Let go… now!" Mardi called.

They tumbled across the maize and came to rest in the sodden ground. "Ugh," Mardi said. On her homeworld, Snook, her unit's repulsor pack would have worked against the iron ore in the rocks. But plants don't have iron ore.

"Well," Perry said, "we escaped the bees."

The Ecori picked themselves up and brushed debris from their fur. "Bee have good memory. Better never go to dungeon again," Asla said.

"That makes sense," Fasool said. He nervously eyed the swarm that was still milling in the distance.

Just then a siren blared.

Asla emitted a high-pitched squeal. "Come with us. Our escape has been noticed."

The five fugitives ran for it. Soon, they were dashing through the marketplace where they had landed. Fasool ran straight for the DAD.

Asla shook her head. "Everything in lockdown when siren go! No can go. No can go."

Fasool skidded to a halt. The marketplace was in bedlam. The Florians and their uniformed droids were leaving no stone unturned in their search for the fugitives. Luckily, the Spartan tourists were clogging the streets, making it difficult to move, let alone look for escaped prisoners.

But as they reached the far side of the marketplace, droid guards spotted them and gave chase.

"Is no good, is no good," Asla kept repeating. She stopped and began swaying as though delirious.

Perry swept the Ecori off her feet and kept pushing his way through the surging crowd.

Behind, he heard Mardi grumble that Tuskan weighed a ton.

Amid the raucous clamour of a siren and the hubbub of the marketplace, some of the Ecori stallholders were doing their best to thwart the droids. Stalls were up-ended, produce thrown, wheelbarrows left across narrow laneways.

The fugitives dashed down an artery. Lost, they stopped to huddle behind a collapsed stall.

"OK," Mardi panted. "Which way now?" She clicked her fingers in front of Tuskan's face. He seemed resigned to his fate. His eyes flickered but his body was shivering.

Mardi swung on Asla. "Which way?" she growled.

The Ecori shook herself. Her jaw quivered for a moment, as though she was trying to speak. "That way," she slurred.

"They're in shock," Mardi said to Perry and Fasool. "I've seen miners like this when their excavations have fallen in on their friends. Come on, before this place clears."

The further away from the marketplace they went, the more the two Ecori recovered. Finally, Asla said, "Down here. We safe."

The Spartans needed no encouragement. They darted down a leaf-strewn vein. Its walls were slicked with a white fluid, which the Ecori explained was a plant food called starch. The next moment Tuskan paused. He pressed against a knob. A narrow entrance appeared. The Ecori pushed the three Spartans through and quickly followed. The gap closed behind them, pitching them into total darkness.

"Where are we?" Fasool said. Darkness equalled deep space. Spartans were never comfortable without some sort of light.

"We in forbidden territory," Asla said. She took a deep breath, as though steeling herself. Tuskan rested his hand on her shoulder and they led the Spartans down a snaking vein.

chapter 5

The Spartans Learn the Truth!

"**W**e are now in section of Flora's original vein. It carry water and sugar before this part of plant dried out," Tuskan explained. "It is where we hiding ever since we learn truth."

"Truth?" Fasool asked.

"Later, when we safe," Asla promised.

A bluish light seeped from the walls. It made their faces appear ghostly as they rushed down the vein.

Then Mardi hissed, "Halt!" She pressed her finger to her mouth, then put her ear to the stem wall and listened. "I can hear Spartans," she said.

"This Trade Delegation room," Tuskan said. "It not safe to linger."

Mardi ignored him. "The Spartans are arguing with the Florians." She frowned. "Flora's charging double the rate for a shared food scheme. Our people don't sound happy."

"Come now," Asla urged. "We take you where there plenty of the proof you need."

Mardi scowled. She just loved to eavesdrop.

The Spartans lost track of time as the Ecori led them down a long pollen tube. Asla stopped at a storage cell and dragged out some breathing masks. "Must wear these soon," she explained. "Otherwise, dangerous to breathe."

Five minutes later, they were all wearing their masks. They reached a platform, overlooking a workstation serviced by female Florians.

Perry noticed something odd straightaway. "There aren't any Ecori down there. Not even the droids."

Fasool shrugged. "So?"

Mardi tut-tutted. "It's odd because the Ecori do

every lousy job on this overblown plant world. And look at the Florians down there. They're wearing masks too. Whatever it is they're handling, it has to be lethal."

She was tempted to take a quick sniff, but Tuskan stopped her from removing her mask. "Is dangerous," was all he said.

Asla nodded.

"Why?" Fasool prompted.

"They produce herb that keep us under control," Tuskan said. "Very powerful."

"Oh-my-stars," Perry exclaimed. "The Florians are keeping you all under medication."

"Is true," Asla said. "Many of us know but are too afraid to speak out. Those who do, disappear in dungeons. Revolution will begin shortly."

Fasool's eyes widened. "What? We've landed smack bang in a civil war?"

Asla put her hands to her face in shock. "No, no violence," she said.

Tuskan took over. "Ecori are not a sub-intelligent species, like most warring civilisation. We simply a spiritual race of farmers. The Florians kidnap us from our homeworld centuries ago."

"And now you're a slave race," Perry said.

"We fought back five decade ago," Asla said.

"But many of our people killed," Tuskan added. "Since that time, our strongest minds taken away. The rest of us they try feed what you see in vats below."

Mardi clicked her fingers. "Which explains why you aren't allowed to eat off-world food. If you do, you'll not eat their tainted food –"

"– and the medication wouldn't work," Perry said, "because foreign food isn't tainted."

"Hang on," Fasool said. Down below a Florian had cut herself. Pale green blood flowed from her veins. She was quickly whisked away by other Florians.

"It's a bit whiffy here," Fasool said. "I almost feel like having a snooze." He readjusted his breathing apparatus, just in case it was leaking.

A sudden blaring noise startled them.

"Is OK," Asla said. "Is their siesta time."

"I almost had a heart attack," Fasool admitted.

"Save it for later," Mardi said. "This is an opportunity too good to miss." She aimed her harpoon at the ceiling.

Fasool grabbed hold of her hand. "You can't do anything," he said frantically. "You're not *Spartan*-born, so maybe you don't know our rules. But it's like this: one of the first laws of our ship is that we don't interfere with other cultures."

Mardi pulled her hand back down. "Oh, really. I read something about that. You have to respect their culture," she said. She looked back

down at the bubbling vats. "Not interfering is one thing, but what these plant people are doing is criminal."

"Hang on," Perry said. "Is it criminal? A crime in one place is legal in another. They say it was like that on Old Earth."

Mardi's face became stubborn. "Leave Old Earth out of this. The place was a toxic waste dump run by Neanderthals from what I hear. No matter which way you look at it, some things are just plain right and others are just plain wrong. And the enslavement of an entire race of people is plain wrong."

"I hate to say it," Fasool said, "but she's right. What about the Ecori laws and customs? Who's respecting them?"

Asla and Tuskan wrung their hands. They were obviously not used to arguing.

Mardi held up her hand and aimed the harpoon again. "You're outnumbered, Perry." Before he could bring the Ecori into the discussion, Mardi launched her harpoon. Its aim was true. "Latch on if you're in for the ride," she said.

Fasool and Perry fastened themselves to her belt and the three swung down to the deck.

Mardi took up some slack as they skimmed centimetres past a dormant Florian. "Drop," she called.

They tumbled across the deck and crashed into a vat. The noise sounded like a drum roll but luckily the Florians were deaf to it.

"I hate those landings," Fasool groaned. He held his head as though it might fall off.

"Don't be so melodramatic," Mardi said.

Perry dusted himself down. "OK, Wonder-gal, what's the plan? I reckon these Florians will be awake in about 20 minutes. And I bet I know what's going to happen to us if they catch us."

"'If' is a little word with big meaning," snapped Mardi. "For now, if we swap fresh water for this green gunge going into the vats, I believe we'll solve part of the Ecori problem." She strode off toward a large vat.

chapter 6

Mardi Fights Back

Perry looked up. Asla and Tuskan were peering down at them. The Ecori seemed to be full of amazement and fear and something like joy. Perry guessed they had been held captive so long that it would never have occurred to them to sabotage their medication.

"Perry, Fasool," Mardi called. "Get yourselves over here."

Within minutes, the three Spartans had swapped several pumping pipes. Clear fluid was soon jetting into the huge vats.

"How much time do we have?" Fasool asked.

Mardi checked her timer. "We'll switch the pipes back shortly and get out of here. With

luck, the Florians won't realise we've made a swap until it's too late."

The minutes ticked by. Finally, the three swung into action and reversed the pipes again.

"Time to leave," Mardi announced. She aimed her harpoon and launched it. "Hold tight," she told the others. Her grappling unit whined at the strain, but it lifted them back to Asla and Tuskan.

"Thank you, thank you," gasped the Ecori.

Then Mardi's mouth gaped. "Hang on. We forgot to re-set the timer."

Fasool's heart thumped. "It's too late, Mardi. Look, that Florian over there. I'm sure she just moved."

Mardi shook her head. "If the Florians guess what we did, all our hard work will have been wasted." She took aim at the ceiling and launched her harpoon. It dug into the ceiling above a wall console.

"I'll be back," she said, and jumped. She landed awkwardly, skidding on the wet surface.

Mardi slammed into the console. She shook her head, dazed. She had landed in the puddle of Florian blood that had pooled after the worker's accident. Groggily, she crawled over to the timer and re-set it.

She looked up and saw the others waving frantically. Sure enough, the Florians were waking from their siesta. An arm brushed her face as a Florian stretched.

Mardi swung the harpoon back to its chute. She raised her hand, fired, and winced when the grappling unit gave a sharp hiss. The harpoon launched toward the opening high on the wall. Mardi almost laughed at the way Perry and Fasool ducked, as though it were aimed at them. But she had seconds before the Florians would discover her.

Luckily her aim was spot on. The harpoon dug deeply and the grappling line ran taut. Mardi stabbed at the rewind stud. She lifted off the ground in eerie silence as the grappling unit winched her toward the others. Perry and Fasool swung her into the opening, not a second too soon. Already the Florians were moving about the deck below.

Perry and Fasool heaved a sigh of relief. Asla and Tuskan wrung their hands nervously, yet their ears were upright with excitement.

Fasool patted his thudding heart. "And we thought coming to Flora was going to be fun!"

Mardi's eyes were fever-bright. "If you don't call this fun, you've led a very sheltered life."

"That's what you think," Fasool said. "We're fugitives on an alien plant world. We've just sabotaged one of its installations. We freed two convicted felons on death row. And if I'm not mistaken, we've lost *Spartan* any chance of reaching a trade agreement with Flora."

"And that's not even mentioning the fact that we've just broken our rules by interfering with an alien culture," Perry added.

"You boys worry too much," Mardi said.

"Is that so?" Fasool yelped.

The others turned. A squad of droids was storming down the vein toward them.

The Ecori stood transfixed, as though caught in the light of a tractor beam.

"Snap out of it!" Mardi cried. She shook Asla. whose eyes were unfocused.

"Get them moving," Mardi told Perry and Fasool.

"What about you?" Perry said.

"Just move!" Mardi shouted.

While Perry and Fasool guided the stricken Ecori down the passageway, Mardi fumbled with her grappling unit. "I hate doing this," she muttered. "But when times get tough..."

Mardi set her harpoon on explosive head and launched it, not a second too soon. The droids' laser pulses were glancing off the walls to either side of her.

Her harpoon found its mark. Its charge exploded on impact with the roof. A tonne of matter collapsed into the vein, blocking the charging droids. A cloud of dust and debris blossomed out toward Mardi. And with it, a surge of water.

"Uh-oh," Mardi said. She ran for her life. She almost crashed into Perry as he came charging down the vein in search of her.

"I heard an explosion and a cave-in," he gasped. "I thought –"

"You know what thought does," Mardi said. She turned Perry around and they ran for safety.

"What does thought do?" Perry asked when he caught up.

"It causes procrastination, silly."

They rounded a bend and found the others. Luckily the Ecori had come to their senses.

Fasool's eyes lit up. "For a moment we thought –"

"Don't say it," Perry said. He turned to Mardi. "Asla and Tuskan know a place where we can hide out until we can make contact with *Spartan*."

Mardi threw a look over her shoulder. Water was gushing toward them. "We'll think about that later. In the meantime, we should get out of here."

"A cell that carries water has burst," Asla cried. She and Tuskan almost reeled. They had already broken more rules than either cared to think about. Damaging a section of the main stem was far worse than escaping custody. Worriedly, they took the three Spartans to a hidey-hole in the main root. They pushed them through the kelp-like foliage that hung over the entrance.

The kelp was foul. The Spartans breathed through their mouths. None of them had ever imagined a smell like this, not even down in *Spartan*'s waste-converter bay.

Mardi nudged Fasool, in case he said something embarrassing.

"Nice place," Perry said, taking up the hint.

Asla's ears stood upright, as though she were pleased. "That is good. Because we must leave you here for long period."

chapter 7

The Revolution

"**N**ow wait a minute," Fasool began. Mardi jabbed him in the ribs.

"How long is a 'long period'?" Perry cut in.

Asla and Tuskan exchanged a hurried discussion. It was full of squeaks and burps, as though they were speaking in code. Finally Asla said, "When revolution begin we come for you."

With that, the Ecori let the curtain of kelp fall back into place.

"Brilliant," Fasool said. "Just brilliant. This is another fine mess you've gotten us into, Mardi."

"Me?" Mardi said.

"Yes you," Fasool said. "If you hadn't come down into the cleaning bay with some Wondergal idea of getting us out of detention, we would've been finished by now and probably fast asleep in our bunks. Instead, you come up with a scheme to spy for Sergeant Zach. And we all know what happens to spies!"

"Of all the ungrateful —"

"You two," Perry said, stepping between them. "Time works differently from planet to planet, ship to ship. If we did our job properly at the workstation, then their revolution won't be long in coming. Besides, didn't you see the level of support we had while we were being chased through the marketplace?"

Fasool clicked his fingers. "The revolution's already begun!"

Fasool was right. They hadn't been in the hidey-hole for more than a few hours when Asla returned. She was so excited that her ears seemed to be elongated.

"It's started," she said.

"What has?" Fasool asked. "The revolution?"

"The change," Asla hurriedly said. "You must come see."

She led them through a maze of veins and tubes to a window that overlooked the marketplace. "It's empty compared to what it was when we arrived," Mardi said. "What's happened to everyone?"

"Most my people all stopped work. They declare station-wide strike."

Perry nodded. "Take away the workers and everything grinds to a standstill."

Asla looked down at the marketplace, where some Ecori were still working behind stalls. "Some are weak and cannot change their way."

"But what's happened to all of our people?" Fasool asked. "They haven't left, have they?"

The thought sent a chill down the Spartans' spines. There would be nothing worse in the entire universe than being stuck on Flora for the rest of their lives.

Asla sensed their dismay. "There no need worry. Your captain call back *Spartan* personnel. Say Flora unstable at present. Will not allow back until everything settle."

"Which it won't," Fasool said. "What if the captain decides to leave? We'll be stranded here."

Asla rapidly tilted her head from shoulder to shoulder. "Negotiation still under way. Just no tourist. No shopping."

Fasool's eyes narrowed. "I don't understand why your people allow the Florians to boss you around like they do. Take a look down there." He pointed.

The others crowded around the window. Sure enough, a Florian was slapping an Ecori with his huge hands. The Ecori was wincing and crying for mercy.

Before Fasool could lose his temper a bee landed on his hand. "Um, everyone, I think we have a prob–"

Asla had been right. The bees didn't forget. A swarm appeared out of nowhere.

"Run for it!" Perry screamed.

The frenzied bees descended on the marketplace. Even the Florians ran for their lives. When the swarm massed, they would attack anyone and anything. Flight was the best defence.

Luckily Asla knew that some Ecori stallholders had built shelters to hide from raging bees. She quickly led them to the nearest shelter and they crawled inside.

Within minutes, the marketplace was dead quiet.

"You should fight back," Fasool said as they left the shelter. "You must outnumber the Florians and their droids three to one."

Asla rocked from foot to foot. She seemed as puzzled as Fasool. "Aggression not our way. Passive resistance always been our way and way of ancestor."

Mardi could see what was going through Fasool's mind. Passive resistance obviously didn't stop the Ecori from being enslaved in the first place. She put her hand to Fasool's mouth. "Your people have done the right thing, Asla. If only other civilisations had taken a leaf from your book the universe would be a better place."

Fasool rolled his eyes. "Which leaves us where?" he asked. "Between a rock and a hard place."

"Hold on," Perry said. "I've got an idea."

✪ ✪ ✪

Asla was surprised at Perry's request. However, she led the Spartans to the negotiations hall.

Perry brazenly entered the hall. The Florian and Spartan top brass were seated, opposite one another, at a large table.

There was an uproar. Several droids drew their blasters and stalked forward. Perry and the others automatically put up their hands.

"Arrest them," cried the Florian negotiator, who sat at the head of the table.

Sergeant Zach and two of his troopers appeared at the back of the room. He shook his head. "There's nothing we can do right now, kids," he said. "You'll be tried under Florian law."

Perry carelessly swept aside the blaster aimed at him. He turned to the negotiator. "We've come to offer you a deal," he said.

The Florian almost snarled. "The only deal we will discuss with you is how much time you shall serve in one of our penal cells."

Just then, Tuskan appeared. He whispered to Asla, who turned and whispered to Perry.

"I don't think so," Perry said to the negotiator. "The Ecori have woken."

The negotiator rattled several stems. "There has been a minor disturbance. It shall be rectified."

"Minor, I think not," Perry said. In a louder voice so all could hear, he explained the situation on Flora. "I've also just heard that the Ecori have taken over the food processing workstation. Which means no more medicated Ecori."

The negotiator, who had just risen from his chair, sat down heavily. "It is the end," he said bleakly.

"Maybe not," said Perry. "Perhaps it's just the beginning."

Epilogue

Three thousand Ecori boarded the *Spartan*. At the request of the Spartans, they took over several of the ship's vast unused caverns, which they converted to farms, solving the craft's food shortages. At the same time, the *Spartan* transported a great deal of automated machinery – including food processing units – to Flora.

The Florian blood found on Mardi's boots was analysed – the Florians had always refused to provide samples for the *Spartan*'s library and database. It was discovered that the Florians were not mammals: they were in fact plants. Indeed, they were extensions of the vast space-borne plant and lived within its cycles. When it slept every five hours, so did the Florians who, like bees, tended the space plant.

All ended well. Except, of course, that Fasool, Perry and Mardi had to be punished...

Plant World Spartapedia

comm.stat. Communication station or intercom.

comp-tute A lesson given by a computer.

Dial-a-Destination jump gate (DAD) A matter transmitter.

Droids Mechanical beings.

Ecori An alien race, enslaved by the Florians.

Florians The indigenous beings of the planet Flora.

Grappling unit Backpack that propels a grapple.

League of Social Conscience An organisation concerned with justice for everyone.

Repulsor pack An anti-gravity device.

Spartan A huge space-faring ship.

Utility belt Multi-purpose belt that has many tools.

Vac-bots Robotic mini vacuum cleaners.